AF485309

The Threadbare Book Of Nightmares

T.E. Hodden

With thanks to Sally Ann, Lynne and Jessica.

For Michelle.

Three Minutes To Midnight

The rain swept in from the coast, and bombarded the small seaside town. The waves were being whipped against the beach, in an olive and foam fury, the crowds driven from the promenade under newspapers and umbrellas. Abandoned deckchairs fluttered and billowed in the wind, while the Punch and Judy man escaped his tent and sheltered in the comfort of the cafe.

Cera White headed away from the beach, into the narrow, winding, streets. Eventually a threshold was crossed, an invisible line in the street where the noisy amusement arcades thinned out, and there were no longer buckets, spades, and plastic balls hanging outside the shops. There were real shops, instead of tourist traps.

Afternoon was on the cusp of evening, and the shopkeepers all seemed to be watching their clocks, waiting to close. Cera was a slave to the railway time table. She had been given the choice of arriving in town early enough to give her time to kill before Lucy and Geoff's house warming, or unfashionably late.

Cera had chosen the former. It was in her nature. Now she wished she had chosen the latter. She was in no hurry to see her friends. To be asked about her appointment with the doctor. To pretend to them that all was well. That there had been a false alarm and the all clear.

One day she would admit the truth, even to herself. But not yet.

She wasn't ready to be seen as somebody waiting to die yet.

Cera paused by one of the shops. The hand painted sign above the door said: Peacoat's Antiques, Collectibles, and Curiosities. The window was full of jumbled and assorted oddities that she thought might be more accurately described as junk. Battered and worn old books, threadbare medals, slightly stained prints, and a tea set that had seen better days.

Cera looked beyond the window. There was a shop buried somewhere under the trinkets and knick knacks. She could just about make out a glass counter, emerging from the piles of jewellery, Toby jugs, piggy banks and statues. In one corner was a stuffed polar bear, in the other a suit of armour.

She was about to leave when she saw it.

A single, framed, card. It might have been a tarot card, but it was a design she did not recognise. A skeleton in a tattered red dress, dancing alone, her hair wild in the wind. Haunting and Beautiful, two things that Cera loved.

She felt a smile twitch at her lips as she went into the shop.

The old man behind the counter looked up at her. This, Cera deduced, must be Mr Peacoat, the proprietor. His face weathered and gaunt, his eyes set deep, a pipe between his lips. His coat, sweater, and hat gave him the impression of a sailor in an old film, probably intentionally, Cera decided, to charm the tourists.

"Can I help you ma'am?" He asked.

"How much is the framed card?" Cera asked. "In the window?"

"Queen Of Shadows," the old man puffed out his cheeks. "A nice piece, if I might say so."

He put a pair of wire framed glasses on his nose and squinted at a hand written label.

"Five pounds. It's... a little worse for wear." He chuckled and held out a hand. "Is it a deal?"

"Yeah," Cera shook his hand, and dug in her handbag for some cash. "I have never seen anything like that in a deck of cards."

"No." Peacoat smiled at her. "I think it is fair to say it is a piece of art inspired by Tarot cards, rather than a card in any recognised deck. An interesting piece, if I say so myself."

"Is it a lucky card?" Cera asked.

"All cards bring their own luck Miss." Peacoat wrapped the framed card in brown paper. "They all have the same chance of being shuffled into a hand. This one happens to be about shared fate."

"Shared fate?"

"Aye." Peacoat handed Cera the package. It suddenly felt heavy in her hands. "They say she takes two souls, and knits them together. When you find the one you want Miss, you wish on this card just as hard as you can, and you won't ever stray too far apart. Bound forever."

"That's nice, as long as you have forever to spend."

"Ah." Peacoat smiled. "That depends on how you want to look at it."

Cera liked that. She was still smiling as she walked out the shop. "Yeah. Now I just have to meet somebody..."

In his shop Peacoat watched the bright young woman walking away, her spring in her step.

"All cards bring luck my Dear," he muttered to himself. "Shame not all of it can be good."

That which comes after.

At three minutes before midnight I stood on the station platform, and watched as the last train lurched into the platform with a hiss of brakes. The doors slid open with a chime and the few passengers stepped out, bracing themselves for the sharpness of the cold.

The station looked the same as pretty much every other station between the coast and London. The same yellow brick building on one platform, and footbridge to the other. The same benches, signs, and wrought iron fences. It was all painted with frost, that glittered like the sea of stars in the clear sky above.

The crowds brushed past me, into the car park and were on their way. The doors of the train closed, and it lurched away with a whine of motors, vanishing into the shadows of the tunnel mouth. I stood still until the last echoes faded away.

I stood on the platform, alone. She wasn't there.

Of course she wasn't there. But I waited a few minutes anyway.

I sat on one of the benches and took my phone out. I flicked the screen until I found the video. The last video of Cera. The one she took of herself while I was talking to the doctor. In the video she was pale and gaunt. All the joy had faded from her face, all her vitality, energy, and colour was gone. She was grey, frail, bald, and still smiling.

"Hey, so... I know what you are thinking. But you mustn't. Promise me you will never think you are losing me. Because...well... I don't think you are. I can't. I have to believe there is more than this. I have to believe that what we had was worth more than a few weeks. So... Here is the thing. I told you once about the woman, the shadow, I saw in Scotland? Remember? I know there is more to this world. I know there are ghosts, and memories, and I know I am more than just these broken cells and mouldering bones. I don't know what exactly is on the other side, but I have to believe there is more. Yeah, I know. You want to think it is the meds, or the cancer, or the desperation talking. But I am always going to be here for you. When you are ready, when it stops hurting so much, when you are done crying and you are ready to believe, go where we met. Platform one. Midnight. I will be waiting."

This was the seventeenth night I had spent on the platform where we first met, at midnight. I had just got off the train she needed to get on. I closed my eyes, and in a few short seconds I remembered the whole long night. She was stranded, cold, alone, clutching a handbag under one arm, and a brown paper package under the other. She had been at a house warming, for friends who had been too drunk to give her a lift to the station. She mistimed the walk home, and found herself in a state. I offered to give her a lift to where she needed to go. It wasn't that far. A few towns over, half an hour's drive each way. She was beautiful, and she wanted to spend the whole drive asking questions, and... I don't know how it happened. I can remember every second of that night, every blush, every giggle, and every second, yet I still don't know what I said, or did, to deserve her asking me out. There was a film we both wanted to see, and she wanted to say thank you.

Somehow, we ended up spending the rest of her life together.

This was the seventeenth night that I felt more alone in the world than I had ever been before.

*

The alarm shook me from my dreams, and dropped me into a bed that was cold, lonely, and only half full. It took me a second to stop my heart breaking, before I could haul myself from the covers, to face the day. I showered, shaved, drank coffee, and eventually felt prepared to unwrap my brand new uniform. The polo shirt and combat trousers were in a charcoal grey, with a corporate logo on the breast. I dressed smart, adjusted my hair, and forced a smile on my lips before I stepped outside to face the world.

The Kingfisher Shopping Centre was a new development a little way out of town. It sat in an abandoned quarry. On the outer edge were the steep chalk cliffs, then there were sprawling car parks, the shopping centre itself was a palace of glass and steel. In the heart of the complex was a parade of bars and restaurants that ringed a vast pond of crystal waters and shimmering reeds.

The car parks were mostly empty. There were vans for the fitters and decorators working in the department stores. The plazas and avenues of the shopping centre were yet to see a crowd. But there were some sets of scaffolding here and there, and the echoes of workmen's radios fluttered up the gallery levels, to the arched ceilings.

Wallis met me by one of the fountains full of silver fish and pink flowers, that decorated the main through-way. He was a tall, slender, man with a military bearing and square shoulders. His sandy hair was clipped short to disguise that it was thinning, and his eyes were heavy and weary. He offered me a bright smile, and a hand to shake.

"You must be Robin?" He asked.

I nodded. "Mister Wallis?"

"Welcome aboard. I will show you to the office." He gestured for me to follow him as we walked down the mall, looking at the stores that were having the finishing touches applied to their decoration. "We are almost ready for the main event, but don't worry there is enough to keep you busy. Everybody in and out has to be logged, and checked. Lots of contractors and sub-contractors to keep track of, and we have already found some light fingered little wretches trying our defences. You have a good team. They won't see you wrong. I know you are being dropped in the deep end a bit, but they say you have been doing good work, and I'm pretty sure you earned this. But, I'm on the end of a phone if you need anything."

"It was Reg Hawker who was running this shift wasn't it?" I asked.

"Yes. It was." Wallis unlocked a service door, away from the parade.

We followed the corridor down to the security suite. Two team members, Jessica and Harry were sat behind a bank of CCTV monitors, nursing coffees, and whispering chit chat. Jessica was slight and sporty, with raven hair and rich skin. Harry was burly and jolly, with a blonde beard and thick glasses.

"What happened to him?" I asked. "Management didn't say much. Just he moved on."

"Moved on," Harry snorted, like it was a joke.

"We think it was stress," Jessica admitted, reluctantly. "But we don't know for sure."

"Don't know?" I felt a pang of worry. "Is he okay?"

"He called in sick, was signed off by his doctor for a month. After two weeks he told management he would not be back and saw out his notice on gardening leave." Wallis picked his words carefully. "You know how things can get."

"Some welcome, eh?" Harry said, with a chuckle.

"We tried to text, or email, to see if he was okay. But he never kept in touch with any of us." Jessica looked at me. "So, your guess is as good as ours."

"Maybe it was the Widow," Harry said, eyes wide, his voice trying to fill the words with pantomime doom.

"Don't!" Jessica chided him.

"Who?" I asked.

"Nobody. A joke really, from the contractors." Wallis waved it away. "When tools go missing, or a door slams, or... You know the sort of thing. Nobody ever made a mistake doing their job, it was always the Widow."

"The Widow?" I repeated. "Why a widow?"

"Because... That is what she looks like, I guess." Wallis shrugged. "When I was at primary school half of Year Five believed that there was a lost girl in the halls who drowned in the fish pond. I don't know how we all decided her name was Grace, or she drowned, from a few kids thinking they saw somebody in the bushes, but stories are like that. In the Centre, we have stories about a Widow."

"Because she's dressed in a long black dress, and a black veil," Jessica said.

Harry gave her an accusing look.

"I speak to the guys, I hear things..." Jessica held up her hands to defend herself.

"Well, she has never shown up on the CCTV," Harry said.

"Or on my rounds," Wallis sighed. "What with there being no such thing as ghosts. Right? They didn't see anything." His voice tightened to that very special tone certain people use when they are marking a company line. "They. Saw. Nothing."

And that was the end of that.

*

It took me four days to encounter the Widow, and even then, I could not be entirely sure I had seen anything at all. Thursday was a grey and dull morning. One of the cameras watching the service corridor between two shops was flickering and pulsing.

I went to check it out.

As I reached the corridor I soon discovered the problem was not the camera. The strip light was spluttering and flickering. I stood and stared at it.

"Harry. It's the light. Call it in as a fault, will you?" I said into my radio.

"Will do," Harry responded, from his desk.

Something moved in the corner of my eye. It was only there for an instant. A shape, on the edge of my vision. A blur of grey just over my shoulder. I turned around, and saw nothing but a clean, white, empty corridor. I shuddered, telling myself it was just my imagination.

It happened again on Friday.

As I walked into the centre, past a staircase I thought I glimpsed a shadow on the wall and the edge of a skirt just vanishing up the stairs and around the corner. I stepped back and craned my head, in time to see a door bang closed at the top of the stairs. I hurried up the stairs and through the door. I was greeted by an empty shop. The floors were covered with plastic sheeting, and the walls were being painted.

I told nobody. But I did wind back the footage. The door slammed on its own.

*

On Monday, Jessica joined me on the routine patrol.

We paced around the light and airy mall. Our footsteps echoed around the empty plaza.

"You spoke to people about the Widow?" I asked.

"Yeah," Jessica chuckled, uneasily. "Why?"

I paused for a second. "Did any of them... really see anything?"

She frowned. "Would you believe them if they had?"

"Yes." I smiled. "I would believe they saw something."

Jessica leant on the railings looking down at the three floors of shops beneath us. She scrutinised me with her big fawn eyes. "Something?"

"Yeah." I rested my hands on the railings. "I don't know if it is a dead person, but in my experience, people have seen something."

"In your experience?" She asked.

"As a copper," I said. "City of London Police, from when I was eighteen, until last summer. I met a lot of people who had been spooked. There was a poor old woman who was sure Jack The Ripper watched her from her garden. Her house was built over an old yard you see, and she was sure this ghostly figure used to stare at her, intently, from the corner of her garden. He would drift across the garden and vanish."

"And did he?" Jessica asked.

"What I found was a leaking pipe under her lawn, and a column of midges." I smiled. "Add a healthy dose of imagination, and you get a ghost. My girlfriend used to believe in ghosts. She had a story too."

"Yeah?" Jessica raised her eyebrows at me.

"Yeah. She was on holiday in Scotland when she was fifteen. Her family had a bit of a party, and she got drunk, so her Mum put her upstairs in this bedroom with a view of the Loch. When she woke up, early the next morning, there was this woman, dressed all in dark colours, watching her from the corner of the room. An old lady, with kind eyes, and a kind smile. Cera wasn't afraid in the least. She sat there, staring at each other for a few minutes, then there was a noise outside. Cera glanced out the window, and when she looked back, the old woman was gone."

"Okay..." Jessica giggled. "How do you explain that one?"

"I can't," I admitted. "I don't know if it was a dream, or a ghost, or sleep paralysis, what ever the rational explanation, I don't know it. But Cera saw something. I could see it in her eyes when ever she spoke to me about it."

Jessica shook her head. "Or a ghost?"

I shrugged. "The point is... I can't just laugh off something like this. I might not believe there is a ghost, but maybe there were enough little things happening for people to need explaining. If there is too much bad luck around, I want to know, just so I can make sure it isn't a sign of something more earthly that might be a problem later."

"I get that, you like to be thorough?"

"I guess I do."

We continued our walk.

"Your girlfriend used to talk about ghosts?" Jessica frowned. "Why doesn't she talk about it any more."

I struggled to find the words.

"Oh. Oh, I am so sorry," Jessica whispered. "She's..."

"I didn't get to spend anywhere near enough time with her," I said. "There was cancer, in her brain. She must have had it when we met, but she had no idea. By the time we had a reason to suspect... she just did not have a chance."

Jessica paused. "Most the guys didn't see a thing. The joke just spread and spread."

"Most of them?"

She nodded, but chose not to tell me any more.

*

I ate my salad in the car. I did not feel like good company that lunch time. I sat with one head resting on the window, watching old videos of Cera on my phone. Little snippets of better days. I felt like every breath was a sigh.

My radio beeped.

"Jack?" Harry asked.

I reached for the walkie talkie. "Go ahead."

"Camera One Thirteen is playing up again," Harry said. "I want to send Jessica to take a look."

"I'm sure you would love to, but it's your turn." I chuckled. "You know the drill."

"She is standing right here..." Harry added playfully.

"Then she can watch the cameras." I clicked my phone off. "I will meet you there."

A few minutes later I was in the service corridor. The same light was flickering like a strobe. I gave it a thwack with the flat of my hand, and for a second it settled down, before beginning again.

"Well, this is just great!" Harry moaned, as he emerged from one of the doors.

"I thought the sparky fixed this?"

"He did," Harry assured me. "New tubes, and new starters."

"Jess, call it in again," I said into my radio. "I don't want to let this place burn down because they missed a loose wire or something."

"I'm on it," Jessica said. "Oh, and it looks like somebody left a door open on the waterfront."

"Great," Harry sighed.

We walked out to the service corridor and down the concourse to the waterfront. The restaurants and bars all looked out over a broad walk, around the large pond. Harry dug a battered carton of cigarettes from his pocket and offered me one. I shook my head.

"Yeah, well," he puffed on his smoke, "don't be in too much of a hurry, okay?"

He climbed up onto the railings, and sat himself there so he could stare into the water, watching the fish.

I left him to it, and went to find the open door. It was slightly ajar, swaying in the breeze. I pushed it to, and locked it, testing the door to check it was sturdy.

"How did you come open, eh?" I asked the door, giving it a good rattle. "You don't just pop open in a strong wind, do you?"

Satisfied with the door I stepped back onto the broad walk.

"Are you done?" I asked Harry.

He looked up towards me, and froze. The colour drained from his face, and his eyes widened. He took a step away from me. No. Not from me. From something behind me. I stood utterly still, and held my breath. I could hear something behind me. The soft, dry, rasp of an airless breath. The whisper of long skirts against the decking. I glanced down at the water, and saw my own reflection, with another, a tall, dark, shapeless form in the water.

I could feel cold breath on the back of my neck.

I turned on my heels, stepping away, prepared to face an intruder, but finding nobody.

"No." Harry shook his head. His laugh had no humour. "No. Sorry, but this... This is not happening."

He ran from the waterfront, without looking back.

*

Harry sat, silently, at the desk, sipping sweet, fresh, tea, and scrolling back through the footage. Jessica tried to put her hand on his shoulder, for a friendly squeeze. He swatted her away, and concentrated on his work. He was reeling back through time, watching us on the waterfront.

He paused the image. It was from a camera on one of the lamp posts, looking down at us. I could see the back of Harry, with his cigarette, and my front as I stepped away from the door to the bar. For a few seconds there was a something behind me. A tall figure in skirts that were a red so dark they were almost black, a shapeless shawl, and a veil. It stood looming over my shoulder.

"See!" Harry shook his head. "See!"

"Yeah." Jessica smiled at him. "And I don't want this to sound like I am saying that I told you so..."

"This... This is...." He swore loudly and slumped forwards, his head in his hands.

"I see it," Jessica whispered. "I just don't want to guess what it is."

*

A university is not my natural habitat. I sat awkwardly by the office, and tried to look like I belonged. Professor Gattis was a jovial looking older man, with an expressive brow, rich accent, and a red sweater beneath his tweed jacket.

"Ah... There you are. Cup of tea?" He asked, as he showed me into the office. He cleared some papers from a rickety chair, and bid me to sit.

"I hear you are the person to talk about ghosts with," I said.

He grinned. "Yes. And I hear you have something to show me?"

"Er, this... My employers can't hear about this. I think they might consider it to be bringing the firm into disrepute. So..."

"Mum's the word," he assured me.

I opened my laptop and showed him the borrowed security figure.

"Well," he whispered, "that is interesting."

"What is it?" I asked.

"Ah." He frowned through his glasses. "I have seen a lot of videos that I have been assured show ghosts and ghouls. I have seen hoaxes, tricks, smoke, flies on the lens, and digital artefacts. I have seen every way there is to have my expectations squashed, so you have no idea how happy I am to tell you that I do not have the foggiest idea."

"Is it a ghost?" I asked.

Gattis tapped his chin with a thoughtful finger. "Well, before we answer that, we would have to know what, exactly, is a ghost?"

The question hit me in the chest. I stared at him blankly.

"That is two questions really." Gattis fixed his eyes on me. "Firstly, it could mean 'what is the thing we think of, when we think of a ghost?' But it could also mean 'what are we experiencing when we believe we have seen a ghost?' The first is simple. To almost anybody a ghost is some remnant of a soul who was once alive. The second question is tricky, because there are many, many, different answers. There are many effects we can prove cause many of the symptoms of a haunted house. The right kinds of sound, just outside of the range of human hearing, is effective, but lighting effect, and some good old psychology to seal the deal."

"Psychology?"

"Yes. If we hear a story about a ghost, if we are expecting to see a ghost then the noise we can't explain becomes a footstep, and the cool breeze becomes a breath. But what is more important is that we go looking for an explanation. We do some research, and discover there was a murder, or a tragedy, or some notable incident in the building. All of a sudden we don't have a vague notion. Something in our head clicks, we see a pattern, and that person must be the ghost! Of course they must! And when that happens we think back, for any odd coincidence or strange little quirk, and we add that to the story too. Soon we have built ourselves a ghost."

"I tried," I admitted. "But... There was a quarry there before. Not a house, a quarry. A quarry that had a few accidents, but no deaths. I just can't find any reason for a ghost."

"I see."

"And..." I frowned and waved my hand. "But this is not light, or noise. This has intelligence. This is..."

"One of the three percent." Gattis cocked his head. "Three percent of cases that I investigate are ones that I can not explain. Now, the temptation is to call them 'real' ghosts. But that is the lazy assumption. I am forever meeting those who talk boldly of the unknown and the unexplained, before just taking the easiest explanation. Science can not explain that strange light in the sky? Who can say what secrets are abound in the universe at large? Ergo it's a spaceship." He tapped the screen of my laptop. "Maybe these, these three percent of cases are the real ghosts, but that could mean they are echoes of psychic resonance, or something science hasn't explained yet, or aliens, or..."

"The souls of the dead?" I asked.

He looked at me. "Maybe."

"I never thought I would say this," I said, feeling cold and hollow, "but I think I would be more comfortable if it was a dead soul."

"We all would. Dead souls make sense. They have a logic to them. They change the rules of life, but they use rules we understand." He looked at the screen. "If that was a dead soul, haunting somewhere it knew in life we could understand the logic. If it isn't we have to ask more questions. What is it? What does it want? Why is it putting a hand on your shoulder?" He shook his head. "We make ghosts because there is nothing scarier in this world than not knowing."

I felt a chill crawling down my spine. It made all my muscles crawl.

"I'm sorry." He looked at me. "We can understand the logic, but how could we ever know a soul existed? Let alone that they can continue..."

I looked at him, but I didn't see him. I saw Cera, long ago and very sick, making me a promise.

"So, does the shopping centre need a cleanse, or an exorcism, or..." I looked at him. "Is there anything I can do?"

"Yes." He met my eyes. "Off the record, I assume?"

"I don't want to have to explain this to my employers."

"In my experience, making contact is the way to go." He met my gaze. "In ninety seven percent of cases it gives people the confidence to believe that either the presence moves on, or settles down and makes peace. For the other three percent...well... it is trying very hard to be heard. Maybe we should listen?"

*

Another midnight at the station came and went.

I went home alone, and lay in bed.

*

"This is not exactly..." Jessica gave me a grin. "If the company catches us doing this, we could be in some real trouble."

"And if a ghost attacks a customer on opening day?" I offered.

Jessica chuckled. "Okay, fair point."

We were on the waterfront. Gattis was setting up some equipment.

"These are Kneale Probes," Gattis said. "They saturate the surroundings in certain frequencies of sound. In my experience the Three Percent find it easier to manifest in these sounds."

He set the device running. It was a black metal cylinder on a tripod. It made the air tickle around me, and butterflies form in my stomach, and ripples on the water. There was a table on the board walk, pretty much where I had been standing when the Widow had appeared. On the table was a Ouija Board, and a single fifty pence piece.

"Oh God!" Jessica whispered, staring out over the water. I followed her gaze. There was a figure standing over the pond. A tall, dark, shadow.

"See!" Gattis' eyes brightened. "One of the Three Percent! Shall we see what she says?"

He span the coin. It danced on the polished oak board.

"Are you willing to talk?" Gattis asked.

The coin moved to one of the icons. It hovered there, still spinning. 'YES'.

"Why are you here?" I asked.

The coin moved, hovering over one letter, then spinning to another, and another.

F.O.R.Y.O.U.J.A.C.K

"Me?" I asked.

It span to 'YES'.

"But you were here before him?" Jessica whispered.

'YES'.

"What do you want of Jack?" Gattis asked.

A.P.R.O.M.I.S.E.T.O.B.E.K.E.P.T.

"A promise to be kept," I whispered. "Oh. Cera."

Gattis looked at me. "And if he keeps the promise, you will go?"

'YES'.

"You will be at peace?" Jessica asked.

'YES'.

"Then we can help you." Gattis looked at me.

'YES'. K.E.E.P.T.H.E.P.R.O.M.I.S.E.

I nodded. "I will see Cera once more?"

YES

The coin fell. The figure was gone.

*

At three minutes to midnight I stood on the station platform. I was alone with my thoughts, but for once my heart was heavy with expectation. I was ready to believe.

The lights on the station flickered, and there was a figure on the end of the platform. Just where I had first seen Cera. Where we had first met. I felt my blood chill as my feet moved on their own accord, carrying me towards the figure. It was a woman, the right size, the right build for Cera, beneath her mess of hair, wearing her hooded sweatshirt and cargo trousers.

The train was rumbling towards the platform.

"Cera?" The name was a whisper on my lips.

I ran to her. I ran to the figure, to the shadow, and reached out a hand to her.

"Cera is that you?" I asked.

She turned to face me.

My heart froze as my hopes vanished, and horror twisted my lungs in a talon grip. Beneath the locks of hair there was no smile, or familiar features. There was something more skull than face, with no nose, dark voids for eyes, and far too many teeth. Fingers of rotting flesh snatched my throat, and crushed me in a grip like iron, as it twisted me from my feet and hurled me away. I felt a surge of panic as I fell away from the platform and tumbled down to the ballast and the tracks, beneath the wheels of the train. As she sent me to Cera.

Three Minutes To Midnight (reprise).

Robin watched the shop, squirming a little under her coat.

"This doesn't feel right..." Robin whispered. "He's an old man."

"And?" Jake prompted shoving her, a thin smile toying at his lips.

"And, he looks, I don't know... poor. It isn't like he is rich is it?" Robin protested.

"So don't steal a bundle of cash, or a diamond, or nothing!" Chris laughed. "A toy, or a book isn't going to make a difference is it? Who gets hurt? Look at the shop! It's junk."

Robin wanted to shove the boys away. She wanted to glower at them, and tell them that it didn't matter if it was junk or not, it was all Old Peacoat had. She wanted to tell them to grow up, and just because junk meant nothing to them didn't mean it wouldn't mean something to the old man.

She wanted to say a lot of things, but all the words caught in her throat and choked her with an angry splutter.

"Do you want me to tell people you are a pussy, or a slut?" Jake asked, evenly.

"What?" Robin felt her fist clench.

"If you don't do this," Chris purred. "Do you want him to tell people you were a scared little girl, who couldn't find her nerves..."

"Or that you let me feel you up in the toilets of the Dog and Duck?" Jake nodded.

"Who would believe that?" Robin asked in a weak little voice.

"What, that you can't hold your drink, and got randy after two pints?" Jake cocked his head. "That you made me promise it was a secret, because you were so eager for me to-"

"You can't say that!" She hissed. "People will call me a slut."

"You will be." Chris shoved her. "To have done a thing like that? Dirty little tramp, aren't you?"

"But-" Robin protested.

"Not her first though, was I?" Jake giggled. "She knew what she liked way too much."

"And what you liked," Chris laughed. "Far too well practised."

"But-" Robin flushed scarlet.

"Go on then!" Jake nodded at the shop. "Get busy..."

Robin glared at the two older boys, and turned to face the shop. She felt her shoulders slouch as she walked into the dingy, musty, shop. It smelt of beeswax and old books. Old memories haunted every corner of the room.

"Can I help you Miss?" Peacoat asked, from behind his counter.

"Just..." Robin swallowed, sure she could feel his old dark eyes trying to burn holes in her. "I'm just looking, thanks."

She stepped towards the corner of the room, and inspected the tray of old toy cars, and action figures. She wondered if any of them would fit in her pocket. She glanced around. She was the only customer, and the owner was watching her intently. She drew her hands away from the toys, and put her hands in her pockets. She tried to look casual, and suddenly could not imagine how she might look when she was casual. She had no idea what to do with her hands. She whistled to herself.

Robin had never whistled to herself in her life.

"They aren't your friends," Peacoat said.

"Pardon?" Robin looked at them.

"Those boys. If they were your friends, if they cared about you, you would just steal that car, or that wolf's tooth for them. You would know it was wrong, but you would know they would only ask you for a good reason, and if they were your friend, you would not have to ask yourself why." He puffed on his pipe.

"Is that legal?" She asked, looking at the pipe. "Smoking in a shop."

Peacoat smiled at her. "You don't want to steal."

"No." She admitted. "But... If I don't they will tell people stories."

"Aye." Peacoat smiled. "And some people will want to believe them."

Robin looked at the floor. "Is it that obvious?"

"Take the wolf's tooth." Peacoat looked at the yellowing canine on the counter. "I will pretend not to notice, at least until you are outside, then I will start shouting."

"Really?" Robin asked.

"Yeah. Give it to the big one." Peacoat leaned forwards. "I don't want you stealing anything that would give him joy."

Robin smiled. As Peacoat deliberately turned his back, she took the tooth, and ran for the door. Peacoat waited until the bell on the door chimed as she bolted from the store, before he turned and started screaming at her to stop and come back.

The three kids ran down the street and into the car park.

"What did you get?" Jake demanded.

"Here," Robin offered him the wolf tooth.

"What?" Chris laughed. "What are we meant to do with that?"

Jake slammed a fist into Robin's face. Another fist crushed into her belly and stole her breath. Robin doubled over., as he snatched the tooth from her hand.

"Useless!" Jake snarled. "What am I meant to do with this? Slut!"

The boys walked off and left her. Robin slumped against the wall of the car park, and sobbed with pain. Eventually she dragged herself upright and slouched away home. As she passed the old shop she saw that Peacoat was watching from his doorway. Not her. He was watching Jake and Chris as they queued in the chip shop.

The smile that Peacoat wore was devoid of humour.

It would haunt Robin's nightmares.

Hot Blooded

"I'm going to have her," Jake said, as he watched Robin slouching away.

"Yeah?" Chris leant on the counter and looked his shoulder, out of the chip shop. Robin was walking away in a huff, still sour faced over the punch.

"Yeah," Jake was full of confidence.

I scooped their chips into bags. The oil soaked youths were oblivious to my presence. They did not see me as a person, I was a part of the furniture.

"You think she likes you?" Chris asked, trying not to sound doubtful.

"She will do whatever I want," Jake said, which did not answer the question. "Or let me do what I want. Know what I mean?"

The pair paid for their chips and started greedily stuffing their faces.

I am pretty sure my disgust at how they were talking about Robin showed on my face. She had been fostering with mum and I for a few months now. I liked her. She had a lot of reasons to be angry, and a lot of troubles under the surface. But she was okay. She tried not to lash out, she tried to be a good kid.

She mostly succeeded.

"Got a problem?" Jake asked. His back was straightening and his shoulders were squaring.

"You shouldn't talk about her like that," I told him.

"Says who?" He looked at me. "A knob like you?"

I shrugged. I glanced sideways. Mum was about to emerge from the back room. I gave her a slight shake of the head. I was okay.

"Do you know who I am?" Jake demanded.

"Yes," I said politely. "You are Jake Harris."

"So, you know who my brother is?" Jake demanded.

Yes. I knew who Doug Harris was. To say that most the population of the town knew who "Dog" Harris was, was not a ringing endorsement of how infamous, tough, or unbeatable in a fight he was. It was proof that our school really wasn't that big a pond, and he threw his weight around. Dog was one of those boys who was always trying to beat respect out of people. He had about four braincells, and all of them were wired into his ego.

Whatever his reputation was, it wasn't respect. It always seemed to me, whenever it was my turn to be shoved around, spat at, and threatened, that if anybody actually respected the fat, blubbery, pimple faced, thug, he would not need to have to waste quite so much time and effort trying to convince people with kicks and punches.

Dog Harris was the reason that we were all forced to sit through a special assembly about how we are all people, and that trying to evict old people from a bench on the sea front park, and calling them a witch, was wrong. I mean... how can you get to secondary school and have to be told that? Who has to be reminded that old people are capable of emotions?

"I know," I said, bluntly.

"Then I say what I want," Chris said, as though I should know better. "And she will do just as she is told. All right?"

"Like what?" I asked, feeling my tone turn cold.

"Like what ever I want!" Jake said, trying to sound aloof. "You'll see."

I glanced at Mum. She was looking worried, her face folded to a frown.

"What ever you want?" I asked.

"Yeah," Chris said, full of bravado. "Whatever we want."

Jake must have decided that too much have been said. "Come on."

He threw a chip at me, and let out a squawk of self satisfied laughter as he stepped away. I tossed the chip in the bin, and looked to Mum.

"Mum?" I said.

"Go find her," Mum sighed. "Find out what happened."

I waited for the Neanderthals to be out of view, then took off my apron and slipped out of the shop.

*

I found Robin by the sea front. She was sat on a bench, watching the waves. When she saw me she sat up and tried not to look like she had been crying. She had a bruise on her cheek.

"Was that Jake Harris?" I asked.

She nodded.

"For somebody who expects people to know who he is, he didn't spend much time thinking who I was," I patted her shoulder. "He said other stuff. That you do what ever he wants?"

"It isn't like that. He's okay." She looked away. "I'm the kid with my Mum. They are jerks, but they are the only friends I have."

"Are you sure you are using that word right?"

"He made me shoplift," she whispered with a wince.

"And hit you?" I asked.

She said nothing.

"Why would he hit you?" I asked.

"Because if I don't he will find worse ways to hurt me," She whispered. "He will make the whole world think... stuff about me. And people will believe it. Because it's about me. People already think I'm trouble. My mum is in prison, my Dad is gone, you can say what I want and people will think I'm messed up."

"You can't be so afraid of being alone that you put up with this?"

"No." She shook her head. "Last term I was afraid of being alone. Now I'm afraid of being ruined and..."

"You could have told me, or Mum, or..."

"I'm afraid of what you will think this makes me," she whispered.

"I know who you are."

She looked at me, and smiled.

"It gets better."

She laughed. "When everybody in school thinks I am a slut?"

"People are smarter than they seem. When I was bullied, I thought the whole world saw me as scum. The stuff they say... They don't believe it. They don't even care. That makes it worse in a way. The kids who say that stuff do it because of what you feel, not what they think. And when that is all you hear, you think the whole world believes it, but it is just the petty knuckle draggers." I put a hand on hers. "The world is full of good people, and they know what those little gits are like."

She shook her head. "You really believe that?"

"I do. It took me a while to see it, because they were piling all the darkness on me, but... Well... How little worth can there be to your life, if you have run out of ways of making yourself look good, and have to try and make others seem crummy in comparison?" I drew a breath. "You will see it too. This time next year you will be in college, looking back, and wondering how you could have ever believed this filled your entire world. You will make a fresh start, and new friends, then seeing how smart you are? University. Don't throw it all away because you think those wastes of oxygen will somehow convince anybody not to judge you as you. I know how easy it is to believe that, but... I won't let you."

Robin snuggled closer. "Why do you care?"

"I know you."

We sat in silence.

"Shoplift?" I asked.

"From a place in town. The guy saw through them. He gave me some little trinket to appease them, then they hit me." She gripped my hand in white knuckled. "I..."

"Don't let them do that. Next time they try and tell you do anything, or go anywhere, walk into the shop. Mum is there, she will look after you. Or if I'm not at college, come home."

That night Robin had a long conversation at home. When it was done, she came upstairs and curled up against me on my bed. I put my assignments to one side, and we put a movie on. Robin didn't find many words. She just lay against me, and looked like she was lost in the film. I could hear Mum, downstairs, making several long and heated phone calls.

Robin looked at me. "The social worker is going to want to know about this."

"Probably," I agreed.

"Great. What if I have to move?" She shook her head.

"Then I will come visit, so I don't miss you."

"You would do that?" She whispered.

"Would you want me to?"

"Yeah."

"Then I would do it." I let out a long breath. "I mean, if they move you too far it would mean learning to drive, but okay."

She nodded. "So... You like films?"

"You noticed?"

"Over the last few months? Yeah. I noticed."

"I do like films."

"So, you know how you always ask if I want to go with you, and I say no?"

"Yes. I do. I am happy to take the hint, and not ask, if you want."

"Would it be okay if I said started saying yes?" She looked at me. "With your friends?"

"Yes," I told her firmly. "It would be okay. Saturday?"

"Sure," Robin said.

She seemed content with that answer. She settled against me to watch the film. Mum finished on the phone, and came up to check on us. She glanced in the open bedroom door and grinned as she recognised the film.

"You two okay?" She asked.

We nodded.

"Okay." She decided. "I have my thing Saturday."

"The thing with that guy from the dating app?" I asked.

"The Detective Sergeant?" Robin enquired, sweetly and innocently.

"Yes. And Yes. Are you two going to be okay?" Mum looked at us.

"We were going to the cinema," Robin said.

Mum chewed on that for a second, trying to work out how much, if anything, it meant. She smiled and toyed with her hair. "Well, if I'm not home, don't wait up for me."

*

The film on Saturday was good fun. Robin still had half a box of popcorn as we walked out into the night. Her cheeks were red, and she was laughing easily. We talked about the film, and weren't in any hurry, so we walked back along the promenade.

"Oi!" The voice rang out. We turned around and saw a bunch of kids hanging around in one of the bus shelters. It was Dog Harris who had shouted. He, Jake, and Chris broke from their little mob and sauntered towards us.

"Where have you been?" Jake demanded of Robin.

"In the cinema," Robin said. "Why?"

"With him?" Dog barged at me with his shoulder. "With this knob?"

"Yeah, he's a friend." Robin spoke evenly.

"He's a knob!" Chris said.

"What is it to you?" I asked. "If you don't mind me asking?"

"He isn't your friend," Dog snarled.

"What?" I asked.

Dog slapped me. "He isn't your friend, because I say so."

"She's my friend." Jake shoved me. "Got it? You don't let me see you hanging of a complete gimp like this again."

"I think Robbie can choose her own friends." I said it evenly.

"Come on," Robin gripped my arm, and we walked away. "I'm not being spoken to like that."

"Don't turn your back on me!" Jake ran at me, and shoved me hard in the back. He curled a fist and threw a punch, that thwacked me across the back of the head. "Come on."

I'm not much of a fighter. I turned, and shoved Jake back, but his brother was leaping on me, with a flurry of punches.

"Don't!" Robin screamed.

"Or what?" Chris asked, laughing.

Robin moved like lightning. Suddenly Jake wasn't punching me. He was screaming like a girl and cowering on the floor, as Dog tried to drag Robin away from her flurry of kicks. The gaggle of kids in the bus shelter were laughing riotously.

Dog turned on Robin, and smashed a fist into her chin to stop her. She staggered back, but Dog, gentleman as he was, followed her with another punch.

I'm not a fighter, but I was bullied enough to know how to not fight. I grabbed Dog by the throat, from behind. He drove an elbow into my face, and I tasted hot, sticky, blood, as my lip split. I twisted his arm behind his back.

"Get off her." I shoved him away. "All of you keep off her. She is going home."

Robin took my arm and we backed away.

"Back off while you are still kids being bullies," I warned them, "and before the police are called about an assault."

"Yeah?" Dog Harris shouted at us. "Yeah? You think this is over? I will kill you for this? I'm... I'm going to get my boys, and we are going to get you!"

He did not follow us. He stood screaming down the street at us, growing red and purple with futile, impotent, rage.

*

I locked the front door behind us, and slipped the chain on. Robin hovered in the hallway, staring at herself in the mirror. She had a dribble of blood coming from her nose. Tears ran down her cheek. Her fist was clenched tight. She looked at me, and her hand opened as her body language softened. I touched my lip and realised how much blood there was.

We walked through to the kitchen. I wet some flannels and we sat at the table, by the patio doors, and cleaned each other up. I wiped the trickle of blood from under her nose, and tried not to stare into her eyes like a puppy dog.

"Sorry," she whispered. "The night was going pretty well, until I fecked it up by... you know... being me."

"You didn't do this," I assured her. The flannel stung on my split lip. I tried to cover by giving her a smile. "He'll think twice about hitting you again, now he knows you hit back."

Her breath caught in her throat. "Yeah, well, today was different. Before he was just hitting me, and... I am pretty sure with some of the stuff I have done I deserve it. But..." She looked at me. "All you did was... be there."

I nodded. "It's not the first time I got hit."

She closed her eyes. "Okay. Ben? Can I admit something?"

"Sure."

"Before I actually knew you," she said, "I kind of knew who you were."

Remember what I said? The school wasn't that big. When something remotely interesting happened, everybody knew.

"When I was in year eight, you got beaten up and shoved in the urinals," Robin said. "I laughed."

"I know."

"I thought it was funny."

"I figured."

"I..." She closed her eyes. "I thought if you let it happen you deserved it. I... I stopped finding it funny when... You and your mum are nice. You don't deserve that."

"It was a long time ago."

"Will you tell your Mum what happened tonight?" She asked.

"When she gets home. We should tell her."

I took the flannel and cleaned the blood from under her nose. I brushed away her tears with my thumb, and she moved her head slightly, letting the touch become a caress. Her smile was small, and raw, full of nerves.

"Are you okay?" I asked softly.

She looked at me a way she hadn't before. The way nobody looked at me. A way I thought only happened in soft focus in movies. She leaned forwards, and my heart missed a few beats as it tried to work out if we were about to kiss of embrace.

The security lights in the garden flashed on. We both turned to see the sea of light that flooded the flowerbeds, decking and shed. We stared at the empty garden. I scanned the shadows for signs of movement, but saw none.

"Just a cat?" I asked.

"Yeah..." Robin did not sound convinced.

She drew away from me, and whatever had been about to happen was gone. She met my eyes for a second, and looked terrified. I took her up to my room, and sat her down on the bed, with something brightly coloured on the telly to distract her while I made a pot of tea and rang mum. Robin opened the window a crack for air.

"They hit you?" Mum asked. "Are you okay?"

"They hit me, Robin hit them, then everybody was hitting. We came home. We are safe. And they are... Bullies is not enough of a word, right? This is ASBO territory?" I asked.

"It's okay." Mum sighed. "I am coming home... If they turn up at the house?"

"I keep the door locked and call the police. Nine Nine Nine. We are safe. We are fine."

"I'm coming home. Give me an hour or so..."

"Mum."

"I'm coming home."

"Okay." I hung up, and took the tea in the other room. "Mum is on her way home."

Robin looked relieved, and stroked the bed, gesturing for me to sit with her. Before I could get comfy the doorbell rang. A fist slammed on the door.

"Robbie!" It was Jake.

We crept to the window and watched Jake looming on the doorstep, with Chris lurking at the gate. Jake was hammering the door.

"Robbie! Get out here!" He roared. "I am not being treated like this! You don't disrespect me! You don't disrespect my family! You will get out here!"

"I'm calling the police," I whispered.

Robin nodded. She followed me out into the hallway and we crept past the front door to the kitchen. I took the phone from the cradle and dialled the emergency switchboard.

"Which Emergency Service?"

"Police please," I said.

"Robbie! Do as I say before I come in there!" Jake screamed.

"Police." The Operator had me confirm my name and address. "What is the nature of the emergency sir?"

The security lights flashed on in the garden. Dog Harris was jumping over the back gate.

"I am going to kill your friend!" Jake screamed through the letterbox. "Kill Ben, and beat you until you beg me to kiss it better!"

"Two youths are trying to get into my house to attack my friend," I said. "They are incredibly violent. Dog Harris and his brother Jake, and another lad."

"Robbie!" Dog hammered on the glass. "Hang up that phone or I will fu-"

The world changed in the blink of an eye.

Something vaulted over the fence from Mrs Wentworth's, and landed on the plastic garden store. Dog Harris stopped shouting at us, and turned to face the thing crouched on the lawn. It was more wolf than dog, with a maw of yellowing teeth, jet black fur, and slabs of muscle that bristled with power beneath the fur. But something about the shape was wrong. The front paws looked almost like hands, the shoulders were broad as a body builder's. The back legs twisted the wrong way as though it could walk upright.

There was an intelligence behind the obsidian eyes as it breathed slowly and considered first me, then Dog.

"Sir?" The Operator asked. "Are you there?"

"Send help. Now. Please!" I croaked, barely able to talk.

The creature threw itself at Dog with a burst of speed. In that instant the lights in the house went black. The line on the telephone went dead. The security lights went out. Even the television upstairs went silent. In the sudden darkness I could see little beyond the window. Dog slammed against the patio doors, his eyes wide, before a mass of fur and muscle dragged him to the floor. There was a fragment of a scream, that was cut short in a gurgle, as Dog was swept away, bouncing across the lawn and into the shadows.

Robin screamed a string of swearwords that would have made a fishwife swallow her tongue.

"Yes!" Jake shouted through the letterbox. "I think Dog got in! Dog! The door! Get the door!"

"Oh the boys!" Robin gave me a pained look, as her heart was torn in two. "They are knobs, but we can't let that happen?"

I ran to the front door and unlocked the dead bolt. As I slipped the latch the door was kicked open, and Jake threw all his weight at it, bundling me to the stairs, and driving his knee into my gut.

"Jake! Stop!" Robin grabbed the burly boy. "Chris! You need to get in here! Dog is hurt!"

Jake was too busy thrashing in her grip, trying to smack me. He didn't hear her.

"Jake!" Chris snapped, lurking on the steps to the front door. "What did they say about Dog?"

Jake stopped and looked back at his friend.

"What do you mean Dog is hurt?" Chris demanded, in a serious tone.

The street lights blinked out. Every house on the street went suddenly dark and silent.

"You have to get in here," I warned them. "Please. And lock the d-"

The lupine shadow flashed through the front garden Chris to the floor. Chris' head bounced on the concrete path, as jaws snapped closed on his neck, ripping it apart. Jake's grip on me slackened. The creature released Chris, who flopped on the floor a dead weight. Chris lay still, staring without seeing, limp and... gone.

The creature took bounding steps up the path, sprinting for the door. I pushed Jake off me, and tried to slam the door, as Robin had the same idea. Long, gnarled and furry talons gripped the edge of the door and tried to wrench it open. Together Robin and I smashed the door closed, hammering the claws. There was a howl of anguish from the creature. The claws withdrew, and we pressed all our weight on the door, locking it with the dead bolt.

An immense weight hit the door so hard it bulged against the hinges. Another and another rang out. At last it stopped.

"What do we do?" Robin whispered.

"The Police are coming," I assured her. "It will be okay."

"What are they going to do?" Robin hissed, eyes wide.

"Stay in the car and call in armed support. When I see the blue lights I will go upstairs and shout at them," I held up my hands. "I don't know what else to do."

We looked at Jake. He was stood still, pale, shaking, and silent. His lips kept moving, but he couldn't talk. I took him in the living room, and sat him down.

"Tea is good for shock right?" Robin asked.

"Yeah. I will make him tea."

"I meant me." She tried to smile, but it froze on her lips as a shadow moved outside the window. Something on the street, or in the front garden, too fast for us to see.

Jake stood, and mechanically pulled the curtains closed. Maybe it was to stop him thinking what was out there. Maybe he thought it was another layer of defence. Maybe he was not thinking at all. There was a sound on the wall. Scratches and grunts. Something moved past the window, and up the wall.

"Somebody please tell me that did not sound like the dog climbing the gutter?" Robin whispered. "Please? Anybody?"

"The bedroom window." I hurried out to the hall and looked up the stairs. Everything seemed still. With my heart thundering in my chest, and my blood running hot and cold, I hurried up the stairs. Only the moonlight through the skylight above the landing drove back the thick, velvet shadows.

Robin followed me, holding an umbrella like a club. Jake followed her, reluctant to be alone.

I paused at the top of the stairs, and watched my room. The window was still open a little. Nothing moved but the net curtain, billowing in the breeze. I hurried across the room and closed the window, locking it firmly.

"What now?" Robin asked.

We checked the bathroom window, then mum's room, then Robin's. I felt like I could breathe again when I was sure the windows were locked. Jake stood, staring out of Robin's window, at the garden. His body tensed. His head shook. He clawed at his hair.

"What have you two done?" He demanded.

"Jake," Robin said firmly. "Jake, listen to me..."

"What? I slap you around a bit so you set a dog on Dog? Some bull dog or something?" He grabbed Robin's wrist. "What did you hurt him for?" He tossed her at the bed, and turned on me, shoving me out into the landing. "Are you some kind of psycho! Do you think you can do this to my family! Just to get her panties wet? I bet that is it! Well, I will kill you for this." He shoved me harder. "I will kill you, and stab you, and rape her, and your mum, and your sister-"

Part of me wanted to tell him I didn't have a sister. Instead I heard myself say, in a calm voice: "It's okay. Robin. Lock your door until the Police gets here. Jake. It's okay. You are scared, and hurting, but-"

"It is not okay!" He shoved me again. "You... you did..."

A shadow fell over us, blotting out the light of the skylight. The creature stared in at us. It hammered its paws on the glass, cracking. With a howl like a chainsaw striking steel, it smashed a paw through the glass, and lunged in, jaws snapping as it reached for us. I backed away, dragging Jake with me. He squawked in fear, and took flight. He ran blindly, knocking me down the stairs, and trampling over me, as I bounced and wheeled down the stairs.

I landed in a heap in the hallways. My chest felt like it was on fire, and there was a stabbing pain in my side. Jake was leaning on the front door. He struggled with the locks, and opened the door. I reached out, and he kicked me away. There was a growl. I craned myself to look up the stairs. It was mistake, it made me realise how much it hurt.

The wolf had lowered its head and one arm through the skylight. It was looking right at us. Jake ran out into the street. He was gone. The wolf was staring at me. There was a flash of blue light, and a burst of a siren, out on the street. The police car rounding the corner stopped Jake running. He froze. The wolf withdrew from the window.

*

The Police had a lot of questions. So did the Paramedics, and Mum. There were several Police cars in the street in a few minutes, an ambulance a few minutes later. Robin refused to leave my side. She told the truth as best she could to Mum, then the Police. Jake did not appreciate all the questions. He couldn't see the Police as anything but his enemy, especially when they were asking about his voice in the background of the Nine Nine Nine call, and the disturbance the neighbours were describing.

"What?" Jake demanded of a Police Officer. "What? My brother is dead in the garden and you want to argue about a little fight? A few punches? Is getting the killer too much effort? You want to have a problem with me?"

"Ben didn't..." Robin's words gave way to a splutter of anger. She gripped my hand.

"I need you to stay calm, and talk to me," The Police Officer said, easing Jake away from us.. "I am trying to help you. Do you really want me to have to lock you up?"

I could see the idea forming behind his eyes.

"Yeah. I do. Lock me up. In a cell." He turned and kicked me as hard as he could. "Go on! It can't reach me in a cell!"

His kick stole my breath in a cry of agony. Robin dropped to her knees, grabbing hold of me and clinging to my hand, as she begged he Paramedic to help me.

Jake was bundled between two Police Officers, and secured in cuffs. He laughed. He laughed triumphantly as he held up his cuffs for Robin to see.

"It can't reach me in a cell, can it?" He laughed. "A few cops scared it off, and I'm going to nick. You... You stay here with the useless freaks." He spat at Robin, as a parting gift. "Slut!"

"Get him out of here!" The Policeman in charge snapped.

The two officers hauled Jake out of the house. He was still laughing as they marched him into the street, into the dancing pools of blue light atop the cars. One officer held him, as the other opened the back door of the cars.

Their lives changed in the blink of an eye too.

The lights on all the Police cars went dark. The headlights, the blue lights, and the interior lights all went dead. The radios on their belts all went silent. Jake stopped, mid-step, and looked to the shadows. There was a blur of movement, and he was snatched away from the Police, by something big, black, and wolf shaped.

They found most of him in the park.

They never did find whatever ripped out his throat.

*

Robin didn't sleep well for a long time. I don't think it's all that surprising she had nightmares. When I heard her get restless I would go in her room and sit in the comfy chair by her bed. I put a hand on hers, and told her she wasn't alone, that it was okay. It stilled her sometimes, most times, to know I was there. I like to think it let her feel safe.

I don't know if it counts as a kindness. It wasn't any effort to watch over her. I didn't sleep much at all, and to be honest, it was nice if one of us could feel safe.

Three Minutes To Midnight (Reprise)

Mister Brown stepped from the train into a veil of rain. The storm assaulted the town in thick curtains, driven on a howling wind, to thrash against the streets and alleyways. He turned up the collar of his long coat, pulled down his cap, and hurried on his way, his satchel resting at his hip.

He took shelter in a coffee house, and hoped to wait for the worst of the rain to pass. He sat at the window, with his tall latte, lost in thought. It was only chance that made him look to the tattered and threadbare junk shop across the street. He gazed at the window, and found his eyes drawn to an LP lurking in the back of the display.

His lips curled greedily as he recognised the watercolour shades of the sleeve. Even at this distance the image of the cover was recognisable. Shamanic warrior women, in animal hide leotards that left little of their supple form to the imagination, armed with flint tipped spears and bone daggers, riding giant bees and wasps, between an alien sky and exotic sea.

Fall Of The Wasp Women was a rare record. It was a hole in many serious collections. If it had been in a real music, or antiques shop, then Brown would have known he would never have afforded it, and moved on. But the dingy little shop gave him hope that some clueless house clearer might not know what exactly they had.

Brown abandoned his coffee and hurried across the street, stepping boldly into the humble little shop. The shopkeeper was in the corner, cleaning dirt from a stuffed bear who had seen better days.

Mister Peacoat wiped his hands on a rag and turned to face the newcomer.

"Can I help, Sir?" Peacoat asked, popping his pipe back in his mouth.

"Yes, the album in your window? The LP?" Brown swallowed down his disgust at the pipe. He tried not to imagine what damage the smoke might have done to the vinyl, or what other bad habits the old fool had meddled with.

"Oh, the Hex Wormwood? Yes." Mister Peacoat smiled like an Egyptian Mummy. Brown was sure the duffer belonged behind glass at the British Museum. "A rare piece."

"Yes..." Brown smiled. "How much is it?"

"Six hundred pounds," Peacot said. "You aren't the first to have asked."

Six hundred? Half what it was worth, but more than Brown could afford.

"For an album?" Brown tried, with his best smile. "Surely not?"

"Ah, but like I said, it is very rare." Peacot held the album to the light. "This was his first album you see. It scraped by in the charts, and did well enough to make a profit, but it was before he went Stellar. And he was only a mega star for that little while before he died. Things like this, the early work that had limited runs, that weren't preserved by adoring fans, are rare, and rare is expensive."

"Well, I suppose I could stretch to four hundred, if it is worth as much as you say," Brown took his wallet from his pocket.

"I can't cut back the price any more, Sir," Peacot said.

God bless the clueless farts alien to the internet.

"Four hundred is better than something on your shelf you can't shift!" Brown laughed. "Come on..."

Peacot's eyes narrowed. "It's worth more than a thousand. Six hundred is the lowest I can offer."

Brown made puppy dog eyes. "I can't convince you to budge?"

Peacot shrugged. "Sorry, Sir."

Harry backed away. "Never mind then."

*

It was late before the shop closed. Brown had come back to the town centre expecting to find the shop empty and locked, but the old duffer had still been fussing around. Brown ate chips, and lurked under a railway arch, still the duffer did not leave. Brown went to the pub, and drank a pint. As the bell for last orders was rung Peacoat entered the pub and ordered himself a pint.

Brown slipped out into the night.

At last the shop was dark, and empty. The windows and door were well secured. The shutters were old and a little rusty, but solid and well locked. The back door, from a weed strewn alley, was less secure. It was rickety, with rot and peeling paint. A crow bar had been enough to rip it open.

The store room was cramped, with shelves stuffed with junk waiting to be sold. The air tasted of graves, mushrooms, and damp paper. Brown pushed his way through the landfill, and to the body of the shop. The moth eaten bear watched him with glass eyes as he opened the cash till, and stuffed the meagre takings in his pockets. There were some rings and medals on a velvet cushion. They too went in Brown's pocket. He grabbed the record, and tucked it in his satchel. There were a few others, that might be worth pennies. There was no point leaving them. He dropped a few watches in his pockets on the way out.

Brown left the shop the way he entered, and wormed his way through the alley ways, and out onto the High Street a safe distance from the shop. He slowed to a casual pace. The last train from town was not until midnight. He had ample time to make his way to the station, without raising suspicion.

He slowed under a street light, and opened the satchel. He lifted the album out and inspected it under the amber light. It was real. He slipped it from the case. Undamaged. It was perfect. Brown smiled to himself as he crossed the road, stuffing the record back in his bag.

There was a blare of horns, and a squeal of brakes. Brown looked up at the oncoming car too late to get out of the way. It clipped him, smashing against his back in a supernova of pain. The kerb rushed up to meet him, shattering his thoughts from his head.

He was dimly aware of the car jerking to a halt. Loud music with too much bass spilt out from the car, shaking the world. Somebody stepping over him, in a confusion of guilt and shock. Two. A guy and a girl. It must have been a girl. He saw her stoop down and take one of the records that had spilt out of his satchel onto the road.

"Help!" Brown croaked, his mouth full of blood.

They did not. They climbed back in the car, and sped away with a cry of complaint from their wheels.

Things They Whisper

Hi.

My name is Cassie, but most people call me Monkey. Monkey because my surname is Monk. Monkey as in Wrench. Monkey Wrench Auto-Repair is my little baby. It isn't much, I rent a workshop on the outskirts of town, I work with two other guys, and everybody assumes my Uncle Sal is the one in charge. We do services, MOTs, and all the usual stuff.

When I filled out the form on the dating app I said my interests were going out, live music, clubs and socialising. Every moment since, I have been pretty sure that was a lie. I do a lot of those things, but I do them because that is what my friends do. I like being with mates, and most people, most the time, enjoy the pub, or the clubs, or whatever. But I love helping Andy restore that rusting hulk of a camper van of his, or taking the bikes out for a ride along the coast, or whatever.

Whatever makes my friends smile? I am okay to share in that. Pretty much anything (but, hey, keep those thoughts clean, romance has its own rules).

Okay, what is it about my life you need to know, so this all makes sense? Well, mostly you have to know about Bumble. He lives in the flat across the corridor from me. He's a couple of years older than me, and he carries a bit more weight than he should, but he's a nice enough guy. He's one of those people I didn't hang around with much as a mate, but we kind of ended up going right past 'mate' to 'friend'. I know the distinction is a little vague, but a mate is somebody you are friendly with, and chat with, and you have that bond. Somebody you will always be glad to see on a night out, and always buy a drink for. A friend can be all those things, but has your back when you need it.

A mate asks what is wrong, a friend tries to help.

Bumble is a friend. He probably doesn't realise it, but he is a good one. I've not always been a good friend back. About six months before the story really begins I realised just how crummy I was as a friend, which is not an easy thing to realise about yourself. But I guess I should tell you about why I was a cruddy friend, to make sense of why I started trying to be a good friend.

The day I moved into my flat, Bumble helped me with the boxes, up three flights of stairs. He made me a cup of tea, and took me shopping for groceries. He said he was going anyway, and might as well help me out. I was... a little short on funds. So he loaded the whole trolley full onto the conveyor and paid for it himself. I promised I would owe him. The next time he went shopping, he asked if there was anything I needed, and I asked for a few bits and bobs. I said I would owe him for that.

I would bump into him now and again, have a cup of tea, and a chat. I didn't always get around to it, and to be honest, I wasn't ever any good at making time for it. Unless I needed something.

In my head, I wasn't using Bumble. In my head I wasn't seeing him just because I needed something. I was seeing him because he loved an excuse to use his fancy coffee machine, and he was always a good person to talk problems over with, and convince me the solution I was thinking of was the right one. So, when money was tight, and I couldn't afford those train tickets to Andy's gig, or I needed to top up my electric meter, I wasn't knocking on his door cap in hand.

And when I said I would pay him back? I meant it. I just... never quite got around to it. I went to Bumble with all the problems my girlfriend, Flora, was too smart to get mixed up with.

I know what you are thinking. I'll be honest: At work, I keep the books even. Everything is billed, everything is logged and tallies, and the bank account always balances, the tax man is always appeased, and I have never had a debt that was not paid by the garage.

In my life? I don't have books, or bills, or tallies. Or my uncle looking over my shoulder reminding me of how much trouble we are in if I don't keep the tally.

About a year after I moved into the building I became single. Flora got sick of all my nonsense and walked out on me. I was not in the best place for a while. I met a few girls, and a few guys, but none stuck around, and nothing stuck.

Andy asked me out, a week or so later. I said yes. We were together, mostly, for three years. Well, okay, there was no real 'asking'. I was working on his camper van, and he got flirty, and when he burned his finger on the soldering iron, I kissed it better, which made him smile in a way that made me blush, and...well... We christened the van three times before we decided it meant we were together. We broke up a few times, over the years, but we mostly worked it out. Andy was an idiot, and we didn't always make the best of it. I had a lot of reasons to have coffees from Bumble's fancy machine for those few years.

Andy walked out on me a few months back. He is in the friendzone again now, and we are both a lot more comfortable with each other now. After all our arguments and fireworks, breaking up was probably the most amicable thing we have done.

But... My moment of clarity came before that, around Christmas, while my relationship was dying a long, slow, miserable, death. I was having lunch with Bumble, moaning about something, I don't even remember what now, when I kept giving him hints of what might make a good present. It was only meant as a joke, wishful thinking really.

"I did have thoughts about that," Bumble admitted.

"Oh?" I raised an eyebrow. "What am I getting?"

"If you wanted, and I don't mean this as an insult, but I could give you a clean slate."

"What?" I lost my appetite in an instant. "What's that meant to mean?"

"All those little debts you owe me, could be wiped away," I said. "I know it isn't any fun, but times are hard for both of us, and you could have a few less things to worry about."

"Oh." I am sorry to say those two little letters were filled with contempt.

I was livid. I was as polite as I could be for lunch, but as soon as I was back in the garage I was red faced, talking like a fishwife, and angry.

"I bought that sod a bottle of pretty good wine, and he fobs me off with this!" I spluttered. "The cheeky little..."

I said earlier that realising I was not a good friend was not easy. It really wasn't. We are programmed against it. Our brains are not wired to see our own faults. We all know somebody who hears the rudeness in every voice but their own, or who can see how vulgar it is for a guy to get vulgar and invade your space, but will do exactly the same when he tries to flirt.

I would warn people away from any friend who wanted a caveat every time you met. The ones who think friendship is a game of give and take they intend to win. I did not want to admit I had been one of those friends. It was easier to seethe and growl, and think that Bumble was insulting me, or indulging emotional blackmail to get me to pay back a few little things.

I expected Uncle Sal to be as livid as I was. But he kept a cool head. He did not ask if Bumble wanted his kneecaps arranged. Instead he came around mine after work and sat looking through the receipts with me. They had been his idea. Sal loves that show on TV with the camp judge in a small claims court. When he realised I had been over my head a few times he gave Flora the book and told her I was to keep a record of every debt I was in, so I could pay it back. To me it had always been evidence that one day I would get around to tidying it up and setting it right.

"Oh, Cassie, this is painful," Sal declared. "It's like death by a thousand paper cuts."

"It isn't that bad," I complained. "A little here and there. I will pay him back if that is what he wants. Maybe then he will buy me a real present rather than a stupid gesture."

"Cassie!" The snap in my Uncle's voice gave me pause.

I instantly regretted sounding like a six year stamping my foot and demanding a real present.

It all added up so quickly. A little here, a little there, and a small favour, quickly became eye watering and painful.

"How good was the wine you got him?" Sal asked.

Okay, I meant to find a way to make it up to Bumble. Life got in the way. There was the break up with Andy, work, and a whole lot of other stuff going on. Don't get me wrong. I was doing my best to be a better friend to him. I wanted my neighbour to think I was good value for money as his friend. I would like to think I did a good job. Things were easier between me and Andy as friends, and that made a lot of other stuff easier.

Then a couple of weeks ago, I had the best idea in the world.

Flora stepped out of her car, and back into my life

*

Flora was my first real girlfriend. The first time it was love. There were people before her. Infatuations, flings, and mistakes. There were people I said I loved, and most of them I believed it for. Until Flora. Then in hindsight, it all looked so cheap and tacky, compared to the late nights, the long mornings in bed, rosy and giggly like we were half our age. Flora could make you feel like you were back at school, and about to be caught fooling.

She was tall, with bleached blonde hair cut short, and a Peter Pan smile. She was the tomboy who would never grow up. She liked to make herself unique with tattoos of flowers on her wrists and shoulders. She carried herself in such a regal way that her hooded sweatshirt and tight jeans might be a ballgown. She worked as a chef, but her passion was music. She was a DJ. She played a lot of retro nights, reviving old tunes with some modern beats and remixing. I don't know if those are the right words. She takes old songs, samples them, and makes new tunes out of them. She can take the words of a dead singer, and let them sing something new, or their old songs in new ways.

I'm doing a terrible job of describing a beautiful thing.

Her car rolled into the garage bright and early one morning, while the kettle was still hot. She parked in the bay and climbed out, smiling at me.

"Hey!" I said, a bright smile on my lips.

"Hey, is this... okay?" Flora asked. "With how we left stuff?"

I answered her with a smile. "Sure."

"I have no idea what else to do," she said, rubbing the back of her neck. "I need a new stereo. The old one is messed up."

"May I?" I asked.

Flora nodded, so I sat in her funky little hatchback, with the body kit and personal decals, and flicked on her expensive stereo. It seemed to work fine. The music was not what I expected. The song was old, soft, and lyrical with a shamanic feel. The lyrics were breathless and husky.

"What's wrong with it?" I asked.

"It only plays that song," Flora sighed. She tapped the screen, chose another album, and played a track that should have been thumping electric beats.

The same shamanic crooning and unplugged strings ebbed and flowed from the stereo.

She tried another album. The same strings and wheezing.

"It might just need a reboot," I said. "Leave it with me, okay?"

"Reset it, reboot it, or replace it." Flora seethed. "I can't listen to that song another time, okay?"

"Okay. And... Hey Flora?"

"Yeah?"

"Are you still single?" I tried to make the question sound innocent.

"Oh no!" Flora laughed and shook her head. "I only want a friend looking at the stereo."

"Not for me!" I squeaked.

She looked at me. "Okay. I dread asking, but..."

"Bumble."

"The one who is all hair, teeth and anoraks?" Flora filled the words with fondness. "Why are you asking that?"

"Because he's single, and you're single, and you two got along fine."

"You got along fine," Flora said with a chuckle. "I remember that."

"Yeah, but I am hard work, and expensive. He deserves somebody who is worth his kindness, like you, and who won't take it for granted, like you." I met her eyes. "But, I'm just making a suggestion."

"Does he still get the overspill of your drama?" She asked.

"I am trying to have less drama, but yes. He is a good friend. He deserves... something."

"And he asked you set him up? On the off chance I stopped by?" Flora giggled.

I shook my head.

"So, what brought this on?" Flora demanded.

"I am trying to be a good friend."

"To me or him?"

"Right now? Both." I felt my chest swell with pride. "Did he have the coffee machine before you moved out? He has a coffee machine. It makes lattes."

"Okay."

"Okay?"

"I will ask if he wants some company, and see if it becomes a date," Flora said. "If it means my car gets fixed. That song is driving me round the twist." She handed me a pile of memory sticks. "My music, in case you have to wipe it all. Okay?"

See. I can do nice things. Flora was all fire, music, and passion. Bumble was all heart, soul, and patience. People think you need to be alike to resonate. That isn't true. When things work it isn't because you are all playing in the same key, it is because you harmonise, and complement each other. You have strengths that the other can rely upon.

By the by, relationships are another thing we can see clearer in others than we can in ourselves.

I reset the stereo to factory settings. I left it chugging away while Sal and I replaced a cam belt on another car. While we were busy toiling, the stereo came back to life. It started playing that same song. When the cam belt was done, I jacked my computer into the stereo, wiped it clean, and recovered as much music as I could from the memory sticks. It scrubbed down, and rebuilt afresh.

But, it still played the same song.

"The thing is cursed," Sal grumbled.

"I can see why she got sick of the song."

"Me too." He rubbed his hands together. "Want me to burn it and order her a new one?"

I looked at him. "Can I try one last option first?"

He cocked his head. "Yeah, well, you want to warn him to expect her call anyway, so go ahead."

I climbed out the car and dug for my phone in my pocket. I wasn't even looking at the wing of the car, just in that direction when I saw the cracks on the bumper. I crouched down for a closer look. The bumper had taken a hit. The hollow plastic had been dented inwards, then popped back out into shape.

It was no big deal. Flora would not waste money getting somebody to replace it, it was a job she could do herself. She probably had one on order, and was waiting for it to be sprayed. But, I made a mental note to offer to order her a new one, if she wanted it at trade price.

*

Bumble sat in the car with his computer on his lap. His face was creased into a frown.

"What's wrong with it?" I asked.

"The operating system is completely bugged and buggered," Bumble said, prodding around with one of his analysis programmes. "Resetting to factory settings wasn't enough. But I can wipe it all away, and start again. Other than that, it would have to be a new stereo."

I let him tinker for a while.

"Don't you think you should warn him?" Sal whispered.

"Warn me?" Bumble looked confused.

"Well, while Flora was here, it happened to come up in conversation that you were both single, so I enquired if she might want to ask you to hang out some time?" I felt my voice lowering.

"Hang out?" Bumble shied back from me. "Okay, but, she realises it will be with me?"

"You have hung out with her before. You two always got along."

"No." He held up a finger. "Hanging out changes with context. What I have done with Flora, and with you, is have a coffee, a chat, and catch up. But hanging out like this is the kind with flirting, and having to impress people, and... I'm me. I'm not impressive."

I laughed and shook my head. "Bumble, you are thinking on this too much. Just catch up, have a coffee, and a chat and... Why would you think like that?"

"Because..." He stared into space. "Because she is out of my league. I'm not even in a league. I'm in relegation, and she is beautiful."

Oh. My. God. Wait... how could I not have spotted this? "Bumble, you... do like her, right?"

"Yes."

"I mean really, really, really, like her?" I pushed.

He looked like he was boiling in his own sweater. "Kind of?"

"Kind of... as in, you were in love with her?"

"A little."

"Why did you not tell her?" I demanded, with a laugh.

He frowned at me. "She was dating one of my best friends."

Oh. Look at that! I'm a bestie! "Bumble, just... be there for her. You will do fine."

His computer chimed. He frowned. "That should not have happened."

"What?"

"The memory won't wipe. There is still a file on there, that just won't die." He tapped the stereo, and it began to play the same old song. "Hey! Hex Wormwood!"

"You know the song?" I asked.

"The Things They Whisper, from the Fall Of The Wasp Women. My dad had that album."

"It's kind of creepy."

"The whole album is creepy. It's a prog-rock fantasy, and all the lyrics are pretty dark and bleak." Bumble toyed with his hair. "I can't get rid of it."

"You are sure?" I felt my heart sink.

"Sorry."

"Okay, I will let Flora know she is buying a new stereo." I took out my phone to text her. "I can see why this was driving her loopy. There was a whole album of this?"

"Hey!" Sal looked up from the bonnet of a car. "Don't knock it! It's a classic!"

I shook my head. "It's old, but this is not classic..."

Bramble shut his computer, and packed it into his bag. He lifted himself from the car.

"You... You didn't have to do this," he said. "For me. With Flora, I mean."

"Yeah," I laughed. "Yeah, I did."

I kissed his cheek. "You take care, okay?"

As my friend hurried from the garage I sat in the office and ordered a new stereo. Sal poked his head around the door.

"What?" I asked.

"If it is such a bad song, why are you still whistling it?" He asked, with a snort of a laugh.

*

Flora was sick enough of the song to give me an open cheque book for the stereo. I found one she approved of, and placed the order, then set about doing other work. The day was busy enough to go quickly. Soon I was driving home. I wasn't really listening to the radio, I only have it on for company. I could not tell you what oldies had been playing for most the journey. But as soon as the opening chords of The Things They Whisper rang out, I swore loudly and changed channels.

I had endured the song quite enough, thank you.

Something finished playing on the next channel. There were a few adverts, then the DJ promised a great song you won't have heard in ages. My heckles raised at the hypnotic mantra of strings. Hex Wormwood began his shamanic chant.

I skipped to the evening news on the talk radio station. For ten minutes I was quite happy I had escaped that song. Before I realised that I was humming it under my breath.

I dragged myself up the stairs, and tried to wash away the day in the shower. I did not sing, or hum, or whistle. I day dreamed of pine forests and open fields. A hot shower, and a cup of tea later, I was watching the news, and contemplating take away menus when I heard it.

The music was muffled, and dulled, but it was unmistakable. I opened my front door and stared across the hall. Bumble is not one for loud music, but I guess I was overly sensitive to the song that I was very quickly learning to despise. Familiarity was breeding contempt. I let out a sigh, forced a polite smile on my lips, and resigned myself to my action. I strode over and knocked on his door.

Bumble let me in, wearing a sheepish smile. "Hello. Have you eaten?"

"Eaten?" I asked.

"I'm practising, in case Flora really does ask…" He pointed at his kitchen. "With her being a chef I thought I better do a good job."

I stepped through into his kitchen. He was cooking something spicy, with sweet potatoes, chicken, and chilli. The smell made my tummy grumble. I found his radio, and turned it off.

"I am really sorry, but after today, I can not hear that song again!" I said.

He looked confused. "What song?"

"The Hex Wormwood one." I gestured at his stereo. "I heard it enough for a lifetime, and I know you like it, and I don't want to be rude but... I can't face it again. Sorry."

He looked at me. "But that was the London Symphony Orchestra."

"What?" I shook my head. "I heard it across the way. It was..." I saw the MP3 player plugged into the stereo, and the album cover displayed on the screen. I crouched and read the track. Holst. The Planets. Venus. "But..."

"I guess the strings do have the same sort of quality." Bumble guided me to a seat. "And you do look stressed."

"It was one of those days," I admitted.

"Have you eaten?" He asked.

"I was getting a takeaway." But boy did the food look good. "And..."

"It was a recipe for two."

"Okay." I conceded. "Thank you."

"Are you sure you are okay?" He asked. "No... money problems or anything?"

"No more than usual," I muttered. "Ugh. Don't you hate it when the same song gets stuck in your noggin over and over and over?"

"Yeah," he laughed. "I get that, too."

We ate. We chatted. I managed to smile. I even forgot about the damned song. Before I went to back home Bumble put a hand on my arm.

"Cassie, if there was something wrong..." He said.

"What?" I was not angry. Just confused. I hope he realised that.

"You can tell me. We are friends."

I gave him a winning smile and pushed him away. "It's just been a long day."

I left him to his life. That night I fell asleep on the sofa, and dreamt of running free in an endless forest, with pine needles under my bare toes, and dew mixing with sweat on my skin. My heart ran fast, and I do not know if I was hunting, or being hunted, but my blood was hot and my senses alive.

*

I got the new stereo fitted in a few days and Flora collected her car. The tune had still been worming into my thoughts every now and again.

"You look happy, considering the bill I am about to give you," I laughed.

"I've been texting Bumble." Her lips drew back from her teeth, and a sparkle appeared in her eyes. I knew that smile. I used to make her smile like that. "I never should have let you keep him in the break up."

I giggled. "Going well is it?"

"Ask me tonight." She toyed with her hair. "He is cooking for me."

Ah. So tonight was the night. Good for her. I was happy for my friends, and yet... And yet there was something restless in the back of my mind. It shifted, wormed, and refused to settle. I made myself smile, and reminded myself I had asked for this. I wanted this. Two friends being happy should not have made me so uncomfortable.

That evening, as I got to the top of the stairs I could hear music and laughter from Bumble's flat. I paused on the landing, smiling as I heard the laughter. I stepped over to his door and listened. Bumble was cooking, and Flora was giving him some good natured teasing about his methods. There was no malice to the jousting, and their humours were good.

The conversation lulled a moment.

"I needed this," Flora said.

"Are you okay?" Of course Bumble was going to ask that. His voice was soft and earnest.

"Yeah," Flora nodded. "I am now."

"Anything you want to talk about?"

"Just the song," Flora said, with a slight hesitation. "It was.... getting to me."

The song. I just realised what song was playing beneath their words. Does Bumble not realise he is being a jerk by putting that song on? I mean if she is saying it got under her skin?

"Did something happen?" Bumble asked, so soft I almost didn't hear it.

"You heard about the hit and run a couple of weeks ago?" Flora asked. "The thief?"

"I heard something about it in the news," Bumble admitted.

Flora takes a few seconds to brace herself for the memory. "I saw it."

What?

"What?" Bumble asked. "You saw it? I didn't think there were any witnesses?" He paused. "You mean you found him?"

"Yeah." Flora's voice was dulled and heavy. "I saw the body."

"I'm sorry." Bumble knew the words weren't enough. "I'm sorry. I had no idea. Here."

They fell into near silence. There might have been sobbing.

"Any time you want to talk about it, I'm here," Bramble promised. "Or, you know, talk about absolutely anything else in the world."

I can't quite explain it, but there was something about Flora's words that didn't feel true. Maybe I knew her well enough to pick up on the cadence of her words. But why would she lie about something so horrible? I was sure she had seen something terrible, the pain was real, and yet...

The restless part of my mind was growling.

I went into my flat, showered away the day, and spent the night channel hopping, looking for a film or show that didn't have that damn song in it. It was everywhere? You ever have a time like that? The first time Flora drove her plum purple car I was laughing, telling her I had never seen one that colour. Of course, some part of my mind made sure I noticed every single one on the roads for weeks after. Or when you talk about a particular actor, and you can't think of a single thing they have been in, then for ages afterwards you see them in pretty much everything?

It was like that. I didn't even know the song, and yet there it was, all over the place, wherever I was looking. I gave up, and watched the news, with my laptop on the sofa playing word games on the internet for the evening.

I heard them in the hallway quite late.

I crept to my door, and watched them through the distortion of the peep hole. Flora lingered in Bramble's doorway, all her body language open, vulnerable, and inviting him closer. He was hesitant, nervous, and mesmerised.

"Thanks, for understanding, for... not making me talk about it," Flora said.

"You should, at some point. When you are ready, it will help." He took her hands in his. He gave her a smile that made his eyes seem as deep as the ocean. "If you want, I know some people you can talk to, in confidence. I can put you in touch with them."

Hey... he never smiled at me like that. Flora had not spared him a second thought since she walked out on me. How comes she can just expect to jump straight to that smile?

"You are sweet," Flora blushed. "Did you want to come find me tomorrow night? When the restaurant closes? I can cook for us, and... we can talk some more?"

"I would like that."

They kissed. It was quick, and a little clumsy. But it made them both melt a little into each other's embrace.

The restless part of my mind buzzed with jealousy. Not so much at the kiss, but at the look they shared as they stepped apart. Bumble looked like Flora had caught a little of his heart on the barbs of the kiss and was taking it with her.

He never looked at me like that, either. Years I have sat by his kitchen table, sipping coffee, sharing all my problems. He never tried to kiss them better. What was up with that? Did I need a neon sign to remind him I was a woman?

Not that he set my hormones boiling, but... a girl can be flattered to be asked, even if she knows she would refuse. Nothing wrong with that.

When Flora finally managed to make her way down the stairs, Bumble gave a disbelieving laugh, and danced a victorious jig back to his flat. The restless part of my mind pined for him, as I lay in bed, waiting to dream of running barefoot in a forest.

It began as a nightmare. I was running for my life, knowing something was chasing me. I could hear it, thrashing through the woods. I sprinted for all I was worth, my toes digging down into the rich, soft, soil, propelling myself on. The air was brisk and cold against my sweat soaked skin. My blood was so hot it burned away the aches and complaint of my muscles.

I ducked through trees, and vaulted across ravines, weaving a path I hoped would be hard to follow. I jumped over a fallen tree and down a steep slope towards a river. At the bottom, I crouched in the roots of an ancient oak, in the blanket of moss.

The figure followed me and slowed to a halt.

Bumble did not look himself. He carried himself tall, and his shoulders straight, his naked body glistening with sweat, his breath heaving as he scanned the shadows. He held his fingers like claws, and his movements were predatory, those of an animal.

He froze, and turned slowly to face me.

I pounced out, a jagged flint in my hand, spinning into a whirlwind kick. My heel caught his gut, and sent him back. I lunged forwards, caught his hair and slammed him back against the tree. Strong fingers clawed at me, trying to hold me back. I knocked them away, and slammed my palm into his chin. He crashed against the trunk of the tree, his knees bending. I pinned him back by the shoulder, and pressed the flint against his throat, until it drew a slither of blood.

"You are mine!" I whispered, my lips brushing his. "Say it."

He breathed hard, and did not resist the kiss.

"Say it," I whispered in a voice like silk as I pressed my body to his, feeling his warmth, and feeling his resistance ceding. "Say it."

He gave in to my kiss.

I woke soaked in sweat and bound tight in my covers.

*

I knocked on the door across the hall. Bumble had a loaf fresh from the bread machine, coffee and home made jam. Breakfast should have been glorious, but my stomach whined for a fry up. His laptop was on the table, he was looking up the hit and run a while back. He caught me looking at it.

"Bit morbid for breakfast reading, isn't it?" I tried to smile.

"Are you okay?"

I didn't know how to answer the question. I ignored it. "What's all this for?"

"Nothing, just... somebody talked about it, and I wanted to know I had my facts straight before I said something stupid. I don't think the conversation is over." He folded the computer closed.

"How did it go?" I asked.

"Oh?" He flushed. "I... Er... It was good."

"Good?" I managed not to sound disappointed.

"It was... amazing." He stared into the distance, into the past. "We just... clicked. You were right. I was overthinking. I was worrying. I..."

For a few seconds I felt my heart lighten at his smile. Then I thought of the way she had lied about her crash, and I felt my whole soul frost over. With her lie, and the dented bumper, I was leaning towards a conclusion I did not much like.

"Damn it," I hissed.

"What's wrong?" Bumble asked.

"Nothing." Well, I couldn't lie to him, but I was not going to tell him I had been spying either.

"You can tell me," he promised. His expression was open and honest. He stepped over and put a hand on my shoulder.

I have no idea where the flash of anger came from. I grabbed his wrist and twisted it. His howl of pain was cut short as my other hand snatched his throat and slammed him back against the kitchen counter so hard the cutlery all jumped. My fingers dug into his throat, pinning him to my will. He tried to pull my wrist away. A knee to his groin took the fight out of him.

He was in my grip. My power. I could take what I wanted from him. I could squeeze the life from him. I could make him listen to me. I could warn him away from Flora, or I could put my lips to his and claim him.

I leaned closer.

The restless part of my mind stirred, dredging up my dreams. My heart quickened, as animal desires burned hot in my heart. I looked at his eyes.

The dreams were wrong. There was no desire. There was no submission. There was fear. There were countless worries.

I let him go, and he staggered away from me. The surge of fire in my veins faded in an instant.

"What?" He stared at me. "Cassie?"

"I..." I stepped away. "I'm sorry."

*

I fled from home and drove in circles until I could make myself go to work. Every channel was still playing that sodding song. Even the Classical channel. The newsreader on the talk radio station was reading the lyrics like poetry.

When I got to the garage Sal had started an MOT and service on a nice old lady's run around. He had his radio playing, (and you can guess what song it was spewing), and a mug of strong coffee. His eyes were heavy with worries too. His expression was far more fatherly than my uncle was usually capable of.

"Your friend rang," Sal said, "asking if you were here, and okay. He was worried."

"We had a..." A what? Oh, Cassie you idiot! What are you supposed to say about this? "We had a fight."

"Over what?"

"A girl." I knew it sounded dumb. "I think I made a mistake."

"Getting him and Flora to look at each other?" Sal asked.

"Yes."

"Because you still like her yourself?" He knew he was groping around in the dark.

"No." I shook my head. "No, I don't want her again."

"Okay, so what is the problem?"

"I think Flora did something terrible," I whispered.

"Okay," Sal nodded.

"And... You know how cousin Bo never liked her train set, and never took it out the box, until I was playing it, then she kept elbowing me out the way?" I flushed. "I think I made a mistake."

"Right." Sal cleared his throat. "Which one did you throttle him over?"

My heart felt so heavy it could have fallen through and shattered on the floor. "Is he okay?"

"He's worried." Sal stepped closer. "I was kind of hoping you would laugh, and tell me he was exaggerating, and I should not be worried, but... You throttled him?"

I backed away. He had that look somebody has when they are about to tell you that you need help, and there are doctors you can talk to. I suddenly felt trapped. Caged. This was wrong. I couldn't be here.

❦

"It was an accident. I had bad dreams and..." I scratched at my head. Anger was boiling over again. The music, the endless cycle of The Things They Whisper, was making my skin crawl. My throat was dry, and raw. "Can we shut that song up?"

I grabbed the radio and put it on the workbench. I gripped a hammer in white knuckles and smashed the damn thing to pieces. Seven good hits and it was in splinters.

"Cassie?" Sal raised his voice, but not through anger. "What is wrong?"

"She killed some guy!" I snapped. "The dent on her bumper is from a hit and run. And instead of seeing prison, she is going to... going to claim my friend's heart. He's my friend. Not hers!"

"You think she killed somebody?" Sal asked, slowly. "Can you prove it?"

"I heard Flora talking to Bumble. I know she lied. I can't prove it yet, but..." I knew how pathetic it sounded. I would not have believed it.

"You don't like the way she was talking to the guy you suddenly make gooey eyes for?" Sal's tone was not unkind. "Want me to look into it, while you stay at mine a while, and relax and..."

"No." My fists curled. "I can't prove it yet. But I will..."

I turned and marched from the garage.

*

Flora's house had not changed since we were a thing. I clawed my way over the back gates into her garden. The spare key was still in a spice jar, hidden at the back of the cool frame in the herb beds. I let myself in through the back door.

The kitchen was spacious and clean, full of expensive toys. I helped myself to a heavy bladed knife from the magnetic rack. It felt right in my hand. A reassuring presence, like the hand of a lover. I made my way through to her office, and tapped open her computer.

It took me a few moments to find the hit and run on the web page for the local newspaper. I checked Flora's social media. She was playing a gig that night with another DJ. Her boyfriend at the time, Speck. Their sets finished around the right time to be driving home and kill somebody. The band took over before midnight. I clicked open her private messages. The ones to Speck had been deleted, which felt more like destroying evidence than getting an ex out of sight and out of mind.

I saw her messages to Bumble. They were sickly sweet.

Bumble: It was really nice to see you last night. Thank you.

Flora: You don't have to thank me.

Bumble: But I can. It was a nice evening.

Flora: It was . I should have asked long ago. You were a mate and I let you slip too far away.

And I am listening to this thinking: See? A mate. Not a friend. What did I tell you?

Flora: And it is good to know I can talk if I have to.

Bumble: Of course. You are a friend. Right?

Flora: Kinda. Sorta.

Bumble: Only kind of? Sorry.

Flora: No. I was thinking maybe we weren't just friends...

Flora: I mean it. It helps a lot. The last few weeks have been bad.

Bumble: Want to tell me what is happening?

Flora: A lot of little things. I lose my temper. I lose my concentration. I make stupid, stupid, mistakes. Nothing you need to worry about.

I left that alone and went to explore the rest of the house for clues. Maybe she would have been kind enough to leave a written expression, or blood stained clothes, somewhere. There was nothing incriminating in the washing basket or living room. There were clothes all over the bed. She had been picking outfits. Probably the effortless kind that made it look like exactly zero time had been spent considering how amazingly well the tight shirt and jeans showed off her curves, and drew the eyes where she wanted them.

I stepped into the sound proofed studio. There was a computer, with a deck for transferring records into digital for sampling, and a bunch of other equipment.

Some of the records were dirty and stained. I lifted one from the pile to look at. Hex Wormwood. The Fall Of The Wasp Women. I could feel the song, The Things They Whisper, as I held the sleeve. I could hear squeal of brakes. I touched the stain, and knew it was blood.

My jaw set. My heart raced.

There was the crunch of a car on gravel. I hurried to the bedroom and glanced out the window. Bumble's sensible grey car was pulling onto the drive way. He got out and hurried to the passenger door. He helped Flora from the passenger's seat. She had a dressing on one hand.

I crept into the hallway and crouched by the bannister. I heard them come in through the front door.

"You are sure you okay to be here?" Flora asked. "Your work is..."

"I'm fine. I can catch up at home." He helped her to the living room.

I tiptoed down the stairs, and paused halfway so I could listen without being seen.

"You are sure?" Flora sounded like she had just been given a pet puppy and some chocolate.

"Let me put the kettle on." Bumble went to the kitchen and raised his voice so he could keep talking. "So... Can I ask what happened?"

"I lost my concentration and grabbed a hot pan without a towel. A stupid rookie mistake." Flora spent a few seconds weighing the truth. "It will sound stupid."

"Try me?" Bumble offered.

"The last few weeks, since I... Since I saw that dead body?" There. You can hear the lie in her tone too, right? It isn't just me? The sound of the lie made my skin crawl. It was like ants in my flesh. Anyway, she continued: "I have found it hard to concentrate. And that song that kept playing in my car? It drove me a little... It really, got to me. Like water torture. And... I keep hearing it. I can't be alone. I can't have a second alone, because the song is there, humming away at the back of my head."

"Actually, that isn't surprising." Bumble came back through with a tea tray. "You saw somebody hurt, and by the time anybody found him it was too late to help. It's not an easy thing to deal with, and it isn't something that goes away quickly. Things like that mess us up, and it takes time to get it straight in my head."

"I'm not mad."

"No." He shook his head. "But, if you wanted to talk to somebody, to help get it straight in your head..."

My feet were carrying me down the stairs. I stepped into the living room. They were sat on the sofa. They became statues. I stared down at the knife in my hand.

"Cassie?" Flora gasped.

"You have to tell the truth," I said.

"What?" Bumble asked, his voice level and kind. "What do you mean?"

"The song won't let us go, until she tells the truth..." I heard myself say. "Please. The lies hurt."

"How did you get in?" Flora asked. "What's the knife for?"

"She killed him." I pointed the knife at Flora. "Didn't you?"

Flora shook her head.

"Tell him!" I screamed.

Bumble stood. He put himself between me and Flora, his hands up as he approached. "Okay. Cassie? Okay. She will tell us. Just give me the knife, and sit down?"

I stepped back, and held up the knife, keeping him at a distance.

"It was an accident." The words fell from Flora like anvils. "I was driving, but I was too busy arguing with my boyfriend. He thought I had been too flirty with a girl from the band. It was stupid. This man came from nowhere, stepping into the road without looking. I tried to avoid him, but it was too late." She looked at the floor. "We had had a few drinks. My boyfriend was sure we would be in so much trouble. I... I wasn't thinking. I couldn't. I was trying to process it. The guy was dead, and his records were on the floor. I don't even know why I picked them up. To steal them? To tidy them away? I don't know. I was a robot. My boyfriend dragged me into the car. He said we had to go. We had to get out before anybody in the world would know what we had done. To just leave it to be somebody else's problem. He drove home saying there wasn't anything else we could do. Over and over, like the song..."

Bumble's heart broke. I could see it in his eyes. He struggled to keep his voice level. "It's okay. I promise... This isn't going to be easy, but it will work out okay. We will talk to somebody. We will tell the truth, and I promise I know people who will help you."

Flora looked at him.

"I'm not abandoning you," he said.

"She has to be punished!" I barked.

"Yes." Bumble looked at me. "Maybe. But she can be helped too. So can you."

"She has to be punished!" I screamed. "She has to be hurt. There has to be death."

Bumble shook his head. "Not like this. Not with that."

Anger flashed in my eyes. It overwhelmed me. It was like a dam breaking and a tidal wave washing away everything that was me, and leaving only this monster. I didn't have thoughts, I didn't have a mind. I had one song, playing over and over. I had the pain and anguish of Flora's confession. It itched and burned like the lies.

I lunged at her with a scream, slashing the knife at her. She rolled aside and it caught her arm instead of her throat, slicing a gouge in her flesh. I changed my grip and raised the knife in a stabbing grip. I would silence her words! I would stop the pain! I would still the music!

Somebody grabbed me from behind. Bumble! I drove an elbow into his chest, and twisted to face him. I was in my dream. I caught him, twisted his wrist away, and pressed the knife to his throat. I shoved him against the wall.

For a moment he froze, at my mercy. I saw before me all the things I could claim from him. I could smell moss and rich soil, pine cones and bark. I looked into his eyes.

"Please. Cassie. Let me get help. Don't hurt her."

The music was deafening. The pain under my skin was scalding. The anger in me was supernova.

I drew the knife from his throat, and plunged it into his chest. His eyes widened, and his mouth opened, but there wasn't a scream, just a gasp of pain and confusion. His body felt like cement on the end of the blade. Then jelly. He went limp, his eyes going out of focus. I drew the knife from his flesh, and he just sagged and dropped to my feet.

The music was gone.

The anger was gone.

The song didn't play in my head any more.

The relief I felt, was... like the purest white light. All the weight of the world was lifted from my shoulders. I was free. It was over. I was released from a nightmare into my own life, my own heart, my own thoughts.

The relief died quickly. It faded and cooled as the whole world muffled, distorted, and faded into the background. I stood shaking, staring at the blood on my hand, at the knife. I looked at my best friend. He did not look back. His eyes were dull. The light behind them had gone out.

I was staring at lifeless, soulless meat. Everything that had been Bumble was gone.

Don't you see? Flora killed a man. She had to be punished. Death isn't a punishment. It is quick It is over in a second. The music wanted her to live with something, it wanted a punishment she would never escape. Now... Now she will spend every minute, of every day, of the rest of her life, knowing Bumble was gone, knowing how he died, and knowing why.

I do too.

But... The music doesn't care about that.

Three Minutes to Midnight (Reprise)

Mister Peacoat stood by the counter of his shop, watching the shoppers on their way up and down the street. His pipe hung from his lips, his dark, shark like eyes were cold and emotionless. His expression was slack and uncaring.

Somebody approached the shop. The boy from the chip shop, Benjamin, was walking directly to the shop, with Robin, the would be shoplifter close to him. They were, Peacoat noted, holding hands. Mister Peacoat straightened up, and adjusted his cuffs. His rubbery features flexed to a friendly, grandfatherly, look.

Robin waited just outside the door as Benjamin stepped inside. Peacoat considered the lad. He worked in the chip shop at weekends and some evenings, but by vocation the boy was an apprentice engineer. A boy of talent. His other qualifications, everything Peacoat needed to know, was found in the look Benjamin took over his shoulder as he stood on the threshold, in the way he considered young Robin.

"Can I help?" Mister Peacoat asked.

"I hope so." Benjamin offered a faint smile. "I'm looking for some silver?"

"Silver?" Peacoat nodded. "I see."

"I don't have much, but if you have anything. Like coins, or a crucifix, or..."

"Fighting a werewolf are you?" Peacoat asked.

Benjamin froze. He shuddered. "What?"

"Just a joke. Like the old films?" Peacoat supped on his pipe. "Somebody desperate for silver, but not fussy what, it... rang a bell. Sounded like one of those films."

"Yeah." Benjamin gave a half hearted attempt at a laugh. "Sorry."

Peacoat considered the boy again. "I'm sorry. I was robbed recently. My jewellery was taken."

"I'm sorry." Benjamin looked at his feet. "That is terrible."

"Yes." Peacoat wore a sad smile.

Benjamin's eyes fell on the shelf of books. Enthusiasm dawned on his face as he crossed the shop and ran a finger across the spines of the books, reading the titles. He stopped as he saw the piles of newspaper Peacoat used to wrap items. He paused, looking at one of the obituary. The picture was familiar.

"Hey! Wasn't this girl in the news? Her boyfriend went under the train not long ago?"

"Yes..." Peacoat sighed. "That is a sad tale."

"She died of cancer..." Benjamin shook his head. "And so suddenly."

"Ah, but it wasn't." Peacoat cocked his head. "Tell me... If she knew she had the disease, and that it could not be treated, or surgically removed, but kept a secret, would that be callous or brave?"

"I'm sorry?" Benjamin was taken aback, and wrong footed. "It would depend why. If she was trying to protect her family, her loved ones, from pain, then I think it would be a mistake, but I do not think it would be callous."

"To me it would seem cruel beyond belief." Peacoat shook his head. "To hide such a thing, as you met somebody, as you let them open their heart to you, to smile as they both promise to always be together." He raised a finger. "Make that promise on a foundation of the truth and it is a blessing. It could be her salvation. It could be the strength she needed to endure, to take those few days and make a lifetime. But... the same promise built on a lie? That is a cruel and wicked trick to play upon a soul. And it will be punished."

"Punished?" Benjamin shook his head. "How can you punish a woman who lost so much?"

"By threatening somebody she cares about more than she cares for herself?"

Benjamin shook his head. "That is a terrible thought."

"Salvation and damnation are two sides of the same coin." Peacoat's voice was cold, his tone hardening. "One can not offer the chance for redemption, for healing and salvation, without offering the same chance for pain, for punishment, and damnation."

Peacoat looked again at Benjamin, then out the window to Robin. He saw suspicion, and understanding in their eyes. Too much understanding for those so young.

"My friend was here a while ago. Forced here by bullies..." Benjamin began.

"You are going to be a good man, aren't you Benjamin?" Peacoat sighed. "I am sorry. There is nothing for you here."

Benjamin backed away from the counter, and walked towards the door. He hurried from the shop, taking Robin's hand as though he was never going to let it go. Neither dared look back at the shop, as they walked quickly home.

Peacoat leaned on his window, supping on his pipe, watching them vanish into the crowd.

www.ingramcontent.com/pod-product-compliance
Lightning Source LLC
Chambersburg PA
CBHW071918120726
48001CB00005B/1778